CALEB & KATE

Caleb & Kate

WILLIAM STEIG

A Sunburst Book · **FARRAR · STRAUS · GIROUX**

To Delia, Nika, Abigail, and Francesca

Caleb the carpenter and Kate the weaver loved each other,
but not every single minute. Once in a while they'd differ about this or
that and wind up in such a fierce quarrel you'd never believe they were
husband and wife.

During one of those crazy quarrels, Caleb got so angry he slammed out of the house hating his wife from top to bottom; and she, for her part, screamed after him the most odious insults that came to her mouth.

Caleb went crashing into the forest by their house, pondering why he had married such a cantankerous hoddy-doddy; but after he'd walked a while, his fury faded and he couldn't remember what it was they had quarreled about. He could only remember that he loved her. He could only remember her dimples and her sweet ways, and what fragrant noodle pudding she made.

Instead of going straight back to put his arms around her and kiss her warm neck, he decided, since he was already there, to look in the forest for oak trees he could cut down later and take to the mill. He wandered farther in the woods, grew leg-weary, and, lying down to rest for just a moment, was overcome with all the greenness and slipped into a green sleep.

Before long the witch Yedida, who lived in a hidden cave in that forest, came shuffling by in her slippers, saying secret spells to herself. She stopped short where Caleb was lying, snoring away like a beehive. "How timely!" she snickered. "Here's my chance to test that new spell Cousin Iggdrazil just taught me."

Squatting down, she touched her skinny thumb to the tip of Caleb's left forefinger and, careful not to wake him, barely wheezed these words:

> *Ammy whammy,*
> *Ibbin bammy,*
> *This is now*
> *A bow-wow-wow.*

And there at her feet, instead of a snoring carpenter, was a snoozing dog. "What a darling spell!" she crowed; and pleased to have worked her day's worth of mischief, the witch departed, swollen with pride.

It was sundown when Caleb woke. First he yawned, then he stretched, then he reached to scratch in his armpit. With his *leg*?! Holy gazoly! His eyes bulged and his big mouth hung open and slavered. Where he should have seen a belt and breeches and a pair of heavy brogans, he beheld the belly and hairy legs of a dog!

He was on his feet in an instant, all four of them. Terrified, he spun around to see what he could see of himself. He couldn't believe what he saw. Of course not! Such things don't happen. Oh no? "This is clearly me," he realized. "I'm not dreaming. I'm a dog!"

"*Now* what?" he wondered. "Well, all I can do is go back and explain what happened." And he began trotting homeward, stunned by his new condition, his tail swinging from side to side. Whatever in the world of wonders was it all about? He was suddenly a dog. True, but he was also Caleb the carpenter. He had Caleb's thoughts. And he was running home to his wife, Kate, wasn't he? Yes, on four legs, and sick at heart.

Night fell and there was a simple moon. Kate, at home, was stumbling from room to room, bumping into furniture, dizzy with dread. She had been at every window again and again, peering out, and had been outside many times, but had seen no part of Caleb.

Had her husband deserted her? she asked herself. No, he loved her; he had said so often. But maybe he was fed up with her. Or maybe something had happened to him, a catastrophe.

Caleb was outside the door just then, reluctant to come in and show
himself. He was ashamed of being a dog. But at last he worked up the
courage to scratch. When Kate held the door open and he saw her pale,
worried face, he scrambled over the sill, thrust his hairy paws up on her
apron, and strove to say, "Katie, it's me!" Only a suffering growl escaped
his throat. He tried again. And again. He could imagine himself saying
"Kate," but couldn't say it.

"Poor, lost animal!" she cried. She gave him some water in a bowl on the floor, and a piece of leftover ham. Caleb drank avidly, but he had no heart to eat. When Kate put a shawl on her shoulders and started to leave, he knew she was going out to look for him, and tried to stop her. He held her shoe in his teeth.

"Stand aside, silly dog," she scolded. "This is no time for games. I must find my dear husband. He may be in terrible trouble." Caleb let her go and trotted gravely after.

All night they traipsed through the moon-laced forest. There was no finding Caleb because there he was behind his wife, with the shape and the shadow of a dog.

At home again in the cool morning, her shoes wet with dew, weary Kate fell asleep in a chair Caleb had made for her, and the maker slept at her feet.

When they woke at noon, Kate searched again in the forest, with the woebegone Caleb dogging her heels, sniffing the ground for no good reason except that he felt he had to.

Then she went into town and made inquiries there, in the tavern, at the post office, in the shops, on the green. Everyone was deeply concerned and would keep an eye out, but no one had caught even a glimpse of Caleb—coming, going, or standing still.

When Kate went to bed that night, Caleb got into his rightful place beside her, snuggled against her dear body, kissed her sweet neck as he'd always done, and sighed out his sorrows. She welcomed the dog's warmth. With him there, she felt less bereft.

She fell asleep with her arm around him, but he was awake all night, wide-eyed, wondering. How could he manage to make himself known to his wife? If he could only tell her somehow that the dog in her arms was her husband! If he could only return to his natural state. Or if Kate could perhaps become a dog. Then they could be dogs together.

Kate decided to keep Caleb. She bought him a collar studded with brass, and she named him Rufus because his fur was reddish, like her husband's hair. She taught him tricks: to stand on two legs, to sit, to shake hands, to fetch things she asked for, to count by barking, to bow. She could hardly believe how fast he learned.

Whenever their friends came calling, Kate would show off her dog. He enjoyed these gatherings, the human conversation, but he didn't like to have his head patted by his old cronies.

Kate grew to love her dog, very much indeed. But, though they gave each other comfort, they were far from happy. Kate longed for her missing husband; she couldn't understand why he'd left her. And how Caleb wished he could speak and explain! He would sprawl by her feet, gnawing a bone, while she worked at her weaving. Often a tear would hang from her lashes, or she would stare through the window and sigh, and Caleb would put his paws in her lap and lick her sad face. Kate would scratch fondly behind his ears, caress his fur, and tell him how lucky she was to have such a faithful friend.

One afternoon in late summer, when Caleb was stretched under a tree reveling in the green smell of the grass, some other dogs turned up and enticed him into a romp. Caleb loved it, but soon quit and retired into the house, where the others dared not follow. He had discovered that being a dog among dogs could be joyous sport, but he didn't want to forget who he was.

The dogs came by a few times more, but Caleb gave them no encouragement, and they stopped coming.

Months passed, in their proper order. From time to time Caleb was drawn back to the place where he'd turned into a dog. He hoped he might find in that luckless spot some clue to the secret of his transformation. He would lie down where he had fallen asleep that day, pretend to be sleeping again, and watch intently through slitted eyes. Chipmunks scurried about in sudden darts, birds were busy in the branches, leaves bent with the roving breezes, a legion of insects hummed. Grasshoppers, on occasion, catapulted through the air. Caleb saw nothing extraordinary. He tried chewing various plants, on the wild chance that one of them might change him back to a man. No such thing even began to happen.

Winter came; snow fell. It was eight months since Caleb had become a dog. He kept warm near the glowing fireplace, dozing much of the day. He watched Kate move through the house, hopeless now about ever being able to reveal his true self. And what if she did learn who he was? Would it make her happier? Well, she would know that he hadn't deserted her; but would she relish having a dog for a husband? He decided she wouldn't.

One crisp, starry night, long after Christmas, burglars crept up to the warm, sleeping house. They deftly pried open a window and stole into the parlor with a drift of icy air. But Caleb was instantly up and barking. He scurried through the bedroom door straight at the intruders.

"Fry this stupid mongrel!" cried the shorter burglar, trying to fend him off. Caleb locked his jaws on the man's arm. The taller burglar seized Caleb by the collar, but Caleb held fast.

Kate, torn from her dreams by the hubbub, saw her brave dog fighting two men and ran to help. She pummeled the one who had hold of Caleb and pulled his coarse hair. He wheeled and flung her to the floor, hissing broken curses through his beard. That very instant Caleb rushed him, hoarsely snarling and showing his dangerous fangs. The terrified thief drew a knife from a pocket in his rags and slashed crazily at Caleb, slicing a bit of skin off a toe on his front paw.

A miracle! Caleb didn't yelp with pain. He yelled the word "Ouch!"
and holding his injured paw to his mouth, he was astounded to find it a
bleeding hand. The thief had cut the toe that had been the finger
through which the witch Yedida had worked her spell, and the spell was
undone! Caleb was Caleb again, clad in his old clothes.

"It's me!" he shouted exultantly. Kate gaped, then "Caleb!" she
shrieked. The thieves, frightened to the point of insanity, dived through
the window and vanished. They ran so fast they left no footprints in
the snow.

Caleb and Kate leaped into each other's arms and cleaved together for a long time.

Much later, when they were able to talk intelligently, Caleb told her, or tried to tell her, what had happened—so far as he knew. What had actually happened they never found out. Like many another thing, it remained a mystery.